P9-AFK-150

DICK KING-SMITH

THE SWOOSE

ILLUSTRATIONS BY
MARIE CORNER

HYPERION BOOKS FOR CHILDREN

New York

First Hyperion Books for Children edition 1994
Text © 1993, 1994 by Dick King-Smith
Illustrations © 1994 by Marie Corner
First published in 1993 by Penguin Books Ltd, London
All rights reserved.
Printed in the United States of America
For information address Hyperion Books for Children,
114 Fifth Avenue, New York, New York 10011.

1   3   5   7   9   10   8   6   4   2

Library of Congress Cataloging-in-Publication Data

King-Smith, Dick.
The swoose/Dick King-Smith; illustrations by Marie Corner 1st ed.
p. cm.
Summary: Fitzherbert, the rare offspring of a swan and a goose,
both finds and brings happiness as the favorite pet of
Queen Victoria.
ISBN 1-56282-658-1 (trade)—ISBN 1-56282-659-X (lib. bdg.)
[1. Animals, Mythical—Fiction.   2. Victoria, Queen of Great
Britain, 1819–1901—Fiction.]   I. Corner, Marie, ill.   II. Title.
PZ7.K5893Sw 1994
[Fic]—dc20   93-6286   CIP   AC

The artwork for each picture is prepared using pen and ink.
This book is set in 16-point Raleigh.

The setting of this story was helped by the fact that during the last world war I served with the Grenadier Guards and was at one time stationed at Windsor Castle. In fact, one memorable night I was the ensign commanding the guard at Windsor and thus responsible for the safety of King George VI and his family.

When Queen Victoria (George VI's great-grandmother) lived there, things were very different. After the death of her husband and consort, Prince Albert, Victoria was as miserable as could be. She dressed all in black, she never went anywhere, and she was as grumpy as a bear with a sore head. What's more, this state of affairs went on for ages, and the old queen became very unpopular with her countrymen. Then suddenly, just before her Golden Jubilee, she cheered up no end, and from then on she was top of the pops.

Why, I wonder? What happened to turn her at last into a happy old lady?

Could it have been her new and favorite pet, the Swoose?

—DICK KING-SMITH, 1994

Chapter One

"Mom," said Fitzherbert. "Why do I look different from all the other goslings on the farm?"

He did; there was no denying it. He was larger than the rest, his feet were bigger, and his neck was longer.

"You *are* different," said his mother.

"Because I'm an only child, do you mean?"

The other geese all had five or six goslings apiece, but Fitzherbert alone had hatched from his mother's clutch of eggs.

"An only child in more ways than one," she said. "I doubt if there's another bird like you in the whole wide world. All those other youngsters will grow up to be ordinary common, or garden, geese, but not you, Fitzherbert, my boy."

"But I'm a goose like you, Mom, aren't I?" said Fitzherbert.

"No," said his mother, "you are not."

She lowered her voice.

"You," she said softly, "are a swoose."

Fitzherbert coiled his long neck backward into the shape of an S. "A what?" he cried.

"Shhhhh!" hissed his mother, and she waddled off to a distant corner of the farmyard, away from all the other geese. Fitzherbert hurried after her.

"What did you say I was?" he asked.

His mother looked around to make sure they were out of earshot of the rest of the flock, and then she said, "Now listen care-fully. What I am about to tell you must always be a secret between you and me. Do you understand?"

"Yes, Mom," said Fitzherbert.

"You are old enough now to be told," said his mother, "why you are unlike all the other goslings on the farm. They are the children of a number of geese, but all of them have the same father."

"The old gray gander, you mean?"

"Yes."

"But isn't he my father, too?"

"No."

"Then who is?"

"Your father," said Fitzherbert's mother, and a dreamy look came over her face as she spoke, "is neither old nor gray. Your father is young and strong and as white as the driven snow. Never shall I forget the day we met!"

"Where was that, Mom?"

"It was by the river. I had gone down by myself for a swim when suddenly he appeared, high in the sky above. Oh, the music of his great wings! It was love at first flight! Then he landed on the surface in a shower of spray and swam toward me."

"But I don't get it, Mom," said Fitzherbert. "What was he? Another sort of goose?"

"No," said his mother. "He was a swan."

"What's that?"

"A swan is the most beautiful of all birds, and your father was the most beautiful of all swans."

"What was his name?"

"He didn't say. He was a mute swan."

Fitzherbert thought about this for a while. Then he said, "So I might be the only swoose in the world?"

"Yes."

"There aren't any other swooses?"

"Sweese."

"What?"

"When there's more than one goose, you say geese. So more than one swoose would be sweese."

"But there isn't more than one. Me. You just said so, didn't you?"

As mothers do, Fitzherbert's mother became fed up with his constant questions. "Oh, run away and play," she said.

But playing with the other goslings

wasn't a lot of fun for Fitzherbert. Already they had noticed that he was different. They teased him, calling him Bigfoot or Snakyneck, and they wouldn't let him join in their games.

Time passed, and Fitzherbert began to grow his adult feathers. Often, as he thought of his father swooping down from the sky on whistling wings, he flapped his own and wished that he, too, could fly. Farmyard geese like his mother and the rest couldn't, he knew—they were too heavy bodied to get off the ground. But swans could. How about a swoose?

And the more he thought about his father, the more he wanted to meet him. So one fine day he decided to go down to the river by himself. He would say nothing to his mother about it but just set off when she wasn't looking.

He had never before been out of the

farmyard, and he was not at all sure what the river looked like, let alone where it was, but luck was on his side. He walked across a couple of fields, and there it was in front of him!

Fitzherbert looked at the wide stretch of water winking and gleaming in the sunlight and chuckling to itself as it flowed along. Never in his life had he swum upon anything but the duck pond at the farm, but this—this is the place for swimming, he thought, and he waddled down the bank and pushed off.

He paddled about in midstream, looking up at the sky, hoping that a snow white shape would come gliding down to greet him.

Instead, he suddenly turned to see a whole armada of snow white shapes sailing silently downstream toward him. There must have been at least twenty swans, all heading for this stranger who dared to

swim upon their river. Their wings were curved in excitement, and the look in their black eyes was far from friendly.

Oh, thought Fitzherbert as the fleet of swans approached, all grunting and hissing angrily. Oh dear, I really must fly!

Chapter Two

As Fitzherbert swam hastily away from his pursuers, he spread his wings and beat them madly on the water in an effort to increase his speed. Harder and harder he flapped, and then he felt his body lift a little so that, instead of swimming, he was slapping his broad webs on the surface in a kind of clumsy run.

Suddenly he was airborne, and the swans, satisfied that they had scared off the stranger, did not trouble to follow.

It wasn't much of a flight, that first effort. For perhaps a quarter of a mile Fitzherbert labored along only a few yards above the water and then, tired out by his efforts, flopped back down into the river.

He looked anxiously around, but to his great relief there was no sign of the swans. Nasty, bad-tempered creatures, he said to himself. I wasn't doing them any harm. Why, my dad might have been one of that lot. I don't know that I want to meet him after all.

He swam on, looking around him with interest. He could see other birds on the water—different sorts of duck and moorhen and coot—and there was a sudden brilliant flash of color as a kingfisher darted across.

There were people on the river, too, in rowboats and punts, and one very long, very thin craft shot by with eight large young men pulling at their oars while a ninth much smaller man steered and shouted at them through a kind of tube he held to his mouth.

"In! Out! In! Out!" he called, and the blades dipped and rose as one.

Fitzherbert drifted dreamily with the current, enjoying the sunlit scene, when suddenly a sharp voice cried "Avast there, ye landlubber, or ye'll run us down!"

Startled, the swoose looked down to meet the angry gaze of a water vole no bigger than his head.

"Oh, sorry!" said Fitzherbert. "I'm afraid I wasn't looking where I was going."

The vole did not answer but swam to the bank. Fitzherbert followed.

"I suppose you couldn't tell me?" he said.

The vole turned at the mouth of his burrow.

"Tell you what?" he said.

"Where I'm going."

The vole stared beadily at the swoose.

"Are you featherbrained?" he said.

"No, I'm Fitzherbert."

The water vole shook his blunt head as though to clear it.

"Tell me something," he said. "You comes sailing along without any regard for the rule of the river and then you goes and talks a load of rubbish. Anyways, I never in me life set eyes on a bird like you before. What are you?"

"I'm a . . ." began Fitzherbert, and then he

thought, Oh no, I promised Mom I wouldn't tell.

"I can't really say," he replied.

"You don't know what you are," said the vole. "You don't know where you're going. Next thing, you'll be telling me you don't know what river this is."

"No, I don't."

"Then you don't know the name of that town you can see, down at the end of the reach?"

"No."

"Nor the castle on the hill above it?"

"No."

"Nor who lives in that castle?"

"No," said Fitzherbert. "I don't know any of those things. I've never been outside our farmyard before. But I'd be very grateful if you'd tell me."

"You're lucky, you are, young fellow," said the vole. "You've come to the right

chap. Now if you'd asked a moorhen, or worse, a duck, you'd have been wasting your breath. But there ain't much that I don't know about this here stretch of the Thames."

"The what?"

"The Thames. That's the name of this river. Most famous river in all England, I'd say. And that town yonder is Windsor, and that's Windsor Castle above it. Now then, surely you do know who lives there?"

"No."

"Why, the queen, of course."

"Oh," said Fitzherbert. "What's a queen?"

The water vole sighed deeply. "She's only the most important person in the land, that's all," he said.

At this point a pair of swans appeared in midstream. Fitzherbert backed into a clump of reeds and kept his head down.

"Now, do you see those swans?" said the vole. "They belong to the queen, they do,

17

like every other swan in the country. Royal birds, swans are."

Oh, thought Fitzherbert, I wonder if sweese are? I bet she's never seen one.

"This queen," he said. "What's she called?"

"Victoria. She's been queen for donkeys' years, she has."

"Donkeys' ears?" said Fitzherbert.

"Why, 'tis ages ago she lost her husband."

"Couldn't she find him again?"

"And ever since he went she's shut herself up in that castle. Always dressed in black, she is. The Widow of Windsor, they calls her."

"How do you know all these things?" asked Fitzherbert.

"I keeps my ears open," said the water vole. "Windsor folk come out boating on the river, and I listens to all the latest gossip."

"She doesn't sound very happy, this queen," said Fitzherbert.

"She ain't. Grumpy old thing, from all accounts."

"Perhaps she needs cheering up."

"Easier said than done. Anybody tries making a joke, she says 'We are not amused,'" said the vole, and with that he vanished into his burrow.

A moment later he stuck his head out again.

"She might be amused at you," he said. "Why don't you pay her a visit?"

Why don't I? thought the swoose.

Chapter Three

Dressed all in black, Queen Victoria stood at an upper window in Windsor Castle and looked down at the courtyard below. In the center of this courtyard was a perfect square of brilliantly green grass, a lawn that was not only personally mowed by the royal head gardener but afterward finely manicured by a number of undergardeners armed with nail-scissors. No other feet were allowed upon this lawn save those of the queen's pet dogs and of the footman who tidied up after them with an elegant brass shovel.

But now it seemed there was a large shape right in the center of the square of green.

The queen held out a hand.

"Our pince-nez," she said to her Lady of the Bedchamber, and when these were brought, she fitted them upon the bridge of the royal nose.

For some moments she stared down, and then she said, "And what, pray, is that?"

"It is a bird, Ma'am," said the Lady of the Bedchamber.

"We can see that," said Queen Victoria. "We are not blind. See that it is removed immediately. Whatever is it doing on our grass?" and she turned away from the window.

The Lady of the Bedchamber heaved a sigh of relief that she had not had to answer the queen's last question. She could see

plainly what the bird had that moment done on the grass.

"That's better!" said Fitzherbert as he wad-dled away from the large squishy mess he had just made.

He was feeling pretty pleased with him-self. Everything had gone perfectly. He had swum on down the Thames, keeping well away from swans, and stopping every now and then to feed on juicy water plants. It was late in the day before he came to the town, so he decided to wait till next morn-ing before visiting the castle.

At dawn Fitzherbert looked up to see its walls and towers looming above. Good thing sweese can fly, he thought, and he took off and flew up the hill.

The town of Windsor was still asleep, and its streets were as yet empty of the busy daytime horse-drawn traffic. Only a

milkman driving his cart with its load of brass-bound wooden churns noticed a large bird flying up Castle Hill and over the turrets of the Henry VIII Gate.

This, Fitzherbert's second flight, was altogether a much more successful effort, but even so he tired rapidly, and, seeing in an inner courtyard below a square of grass, he landed thankfully upon it. It was a crash landing that knocked the wind out of him, and for some time he lay there and gasped for breath.

Finally recovered, he looked about him. Then he saw movement at an upper window. Someone was looking down at him. He could not see the figure clearly, but it appeared to be dressed in black!

If that's the queen, thought Fitzherbert, I'd better make myself comfortable before I meet her, and he stood up and suited his actions to his words.

"That's better!" he said, and he waddled off toward the nearest door.

The Lady of the Bedchamber lost no time in contacting the lord steward of Her Majesty's household.

"There's a large bird," she said to him, "in the queen's private courtyard, and she wants it removed immediately."

"What sort of bird?" asked the lord steward.

"I don't know," said the Lady of the Bedchamber. "It was something like a swan. But then again it was something like a goose."

The lord steward of Her Majesty's household sent for the royal ornithologist.

"There's a large bird," he said, "in Her Majesty's private courtyard. Get rid of it, will you?"

"What sort of bird?" asked the royal ornithologist.

"Part swan, part goose, apparently."

"Part swan, part goose!" murmured the royal ornithologist excitedly to himself as he hurried to do the lord steward's bidding. "Could it be? Could it be? . . ."

When the door into the courtyard opened, Fitzherbert was disappointed to see a man emerge. He seemed a nice man, however, for he produced some pieces of bread that he offered to the swoose. But no sooner had Fitzherbert begun to eat them than he was grabbed, his wings pinned to his side, and carried away, kicking and struggling.

"It is! It is!" said the royal ornithologist as he listened to his captive's cries of protest, a blend of the grunting bark of an angry swan and the cackling of an outraged goose. He carried Fitzherbert to the royal menagerie, where were housed all manner of creatures presented as gifts to the queen by visiting foreign potentates.

"It is!" said the royal ornithologist again as he feasted his eyes upon Fitzherbert, now shut in a large cage. "I had heard tales of such a bird but never thought I would see one! It is a swoose!"

"That bird," said the lord steward of Her Majesty's household later. "Have you dealt with it?"

"Yes," said the royal ornithologist.

"What was it?"

"It is a swoose!" said the royal ornithologist. "A hybrid between a swan and a goose! A rara avis indeed! Her Majesty should be told."

The lord steward of Her Majesty's household remembered enough of his Latin to say to the Lady of the Bedchamber, "It's a rare bird, that one that was in the queen's courtyard. Called a swoose apparently. Her Majesty should be told."

Nervously, the Lady of the Bedchamber approached her sovereign. The queen did not like to be told things, preferring that people should not speak until they were spoken to.

"Forgive me, Your Majesty," she said, "but that bird that you saw earlier this morning . . ."

"Well?" said the queen, her face set in its usual grim mode.

"I am given to understand, Ma'am, that it is a swoose."

"A what?"

"A swoose, Ma'am."

To the great astonishment of the Lady of the Bedchamber, something that might almost have been called a small smile appeared on the royal visage. Never in all the many years she had served at court had the Lady of the Bedchamber seen such a thing.

"A swoose," said Queen Victoria. "Why, surely that must be part swan, part goose!"

"Perhaps Your Majesty might care to see the creature?" said the Lady of the Bedchamber.

"We would," said the queen.

So it was that Fitzherbert, puzzled and angry at his confinement, saw a pair of bewigged footmen open the doors of the royal menagerie and a procession enter.

Flanked by the lord steward and the royal ornithologist, followed by the Lady of the Bedchamber, and attended by the lord chamberlain, the comptroller of Her Majesty's household, the master of the horse, and several ladies-in-waiting, came a short dumpy figure, dressed all in black.

For some time Queen Victoria stared at

Fitzherbert without speaking. Naturally no one else spoke.

Then the queen said, "Are we right? Is this bird indeed half swan and half goose?"

"Your Majesty is perfectly correct," said the royal ornithologist.

"And it is a rarity?"

"Indeed, Ma'am."

"We do not like to see it so confined. Open the door of its cage."

"But Ma'am . . ." began the royal ornithologist, fearing that the bird might misbehave itself in some way, might even (dreadful thought) peck the royal ankles.

"Do as we say," snapped the queen, "and look sharp about it." And the royal ornithologist looked very sharp indeed.

Fitzherbert could, of course, understand nothing of the medley of sounds that the humans made. But it was clear to him that, thanks to the queen, he was to be a prisoner no longer, and it occurred to him that he should show his gratitude.

With measured tread he walked out of the cage and stood at attention before the queen. Then he slowly uncurled his long neck and laid his head upon the ground at the very feet of the monarch in a gesture that was the nearest he could achieve to a courtly bow.

To the amazement of the lord steward of Her Majesty's household and the royal ornithologist and the Lady of the Bedchamber and the lord chamberlain and the comptroller of Her Majesty's household and the master of the horse and the ladies-in-waiting and the two bewigged footmen, none of whom recalled ever seeing such a phenomenon before, Queen Victoria looked down at the swoose and smiled broadly.

"We are amused," said the Widow of Windsor.

Chapter Four

You may suppose that from that moment on, life was blissful for Fitzherbert the swoose. The news that he had made the queen smile for the first time in a quarter of a century—or, in other words, since the death of her husband, Prince Albert— spread like wildfire among the courtiers at Windsor Castle. Not only had she smiled once but she also had continued to do so on occasion and had spoken quite pleas- antly to a number of people. She had even exchanged her widow's cap of black for one of white lace. And all because of the swoose!

A number of measures were now taken for Fitzherbert's comfort and to ensure that he did not depart. To make certain that he stayed, the royal ornithologist clipped the flight feathers of one of his wings, thus rendering him incapable of flying. This was not necessary, however, since Fitzherbert had no intention of going. He knew when he was on to a good thing.

Being the favorite of the queen meant, for example, that he was offered only the choicest food, such as fresh young vegetables from the kitchen gardens brought to him by the royal head gardener in person, and Scotch oatmeal porridge served by the queen's manservant, John Brown.

In addition, the royal head gardener's little daughter was appointed swoosegirl-in-waiting and took Fitzherbert for daily

walks in Windsor Great Park. By night, however, he was shut in the royal menagerie for his own safety (for foxes, the royal ornithologist was sure, would be no respecters of sweese), but the queen came in each evening to see her pet. Fitzherbert would make his bow, the queen would smile, and everyone would heave a sigh of relief at the welcome change that had come over the crusty old lady.

"It's all so beautifully timed," the lord steward of Her Majesty's household said to the Lady of the Bedchamber. "Next year it's the queen's Golden Jubilee, as you know, when she will have to go about and show herself to the people. How pleased they will be to see her wearing a happy face again after all those years of gloom."

To the royal ornithologist he said almost daily, "The swoose is well, I trust?"

"Oh yes. And he is the apple of the queen's eye."

"I know. Nothing must happen to him."

But something very nearly did.

It all began with the departure from Windsor Castle of the head cook and bottle washer. For years he had served the royal family and their retainers heavy and indigestible meals of Scotch beef or Welsh mutton or Wiltshire bacon or York ham, accompanied by mounds of overcooked vegetables and lashings of thick greasy gravy, and the lord steward of Her Majesty's household had longed for him to retire.

Immediately he replaced him with a French chef.

Soon after this, some foreign cousins of the queen were due to stay at the castle, and the new chef was instructed to plan a modest ten-course dinner for the visitors.

"And make sure that the main course is something really spectacular," said the lord steward.

The French chef sought the advice of the queen's butler.

"Ees zere somezing," he asked, "zat only royalty may eat?"

The queen's butler thought for a moment.

"Why yes," he said, "there is. Swan. Royal birds, swans are. No one else is allowed to eat them. There are plenty down there on the Thames."

Roast swan and all ze trimmings, thought the chef. Zat will indeed be spectaculaire!

All might yet have been well had not the chef lost his way in the many halls and corridors of the castle. One morning he was taking the largest of his carving knives to be sharpened at the armory when he failed to understand the directions given him and became confused in the labyrinth of passages.

Opening a door, he found himself in an enclosed courtyard, in the center of which was a perfect square of brilliantly green grass. Right in the middle of it was a large shape.

The chef's hand tightened on his carving knife.

"Voilà!" he said softly. "No need to go to ze river. Ze bird 'as come to me!"

Fitzherbert was resting, a little tired after his daily walk. The swoosegirl-in-waiting had gone home to tea, and the royal ornithologist had not yet arrived to take the queen's pet to the menagerie for the night.

Suddenly the swoose looked up to see a man approaching, a man dressed all in white and wearing a tall white hat—a man holding a huge knife! At that very moment Queen Victoria, leaning upon the arm of the Lady of the Bedchamber, emerged from a door at the opposite side of the courtyard.

Grunting, barking, cackling at the top of his voice, flapping his wings wildly, Fitzherbert dashed toward the queen and turned and stood in front of her, his eyes fixed in horror on that dreadful carving knife destined, he was sure, for his throat.

Then, drawn by the terrible noise that the swoose was making, a host of people appeared and fell upon the wretched chef and dragged him away.

Later that evening, when all had been explained (and the luckless chef sent hurriedly back to France), the queen came with

her retinue into the menagerie. They brought a gilded chair for her, and she sat and looked at her swoose.

"What courage!" she said quietly. "Not only did he sound the alarm, but he stood before us, thinking that we were to be murdered. He believed that he was saving us!"

Everyone looked at everyone else, but nobody said anything.

"We shall reward him for his bravery," said the queen, and those nearest could see that her old eyes were twinkling.

"Open the door of the cage," she commanded, and they opened it.

Fitzherbert stepped forward and stood at attention before the monarch's chair, and then, as always, lowered his head to the floor.

The queen looked around at her courtiers, and she positively grinned. Then she raised her silver-headed ebony walking stick, and with it she lightly touched Fitz-herbert upon one shoulder.

"I dub thee knight!" said Queen Victoria in a loud voice. "Arise, Sir Swoose!"

And slowly, proudly, to a burst of clapping from the smiling company of watchers, Fitzherbert arose.

DICK KING-SMITH has written many highly acclaimed books for young readers, including *Babe, the Gallant Pig*, which was chosen as a Boston Globe–Horn Book Award Honor book. His previous book for Hyperion, *The Cuckoo Child*, was described by *Publishers Weekly* as "a harmonious blend of poignant and rib-tickling scenes, in which human and animal characterizations are crafted with equal skill and originality." Mr. King-Smith was born and raised in Gloucestershire, England, where he still resides.